Santa's Snow Cat

By Sue Stainton

Illustrated by Anne Mortimer

HARPERCOLLINS*PUBLISHERS*

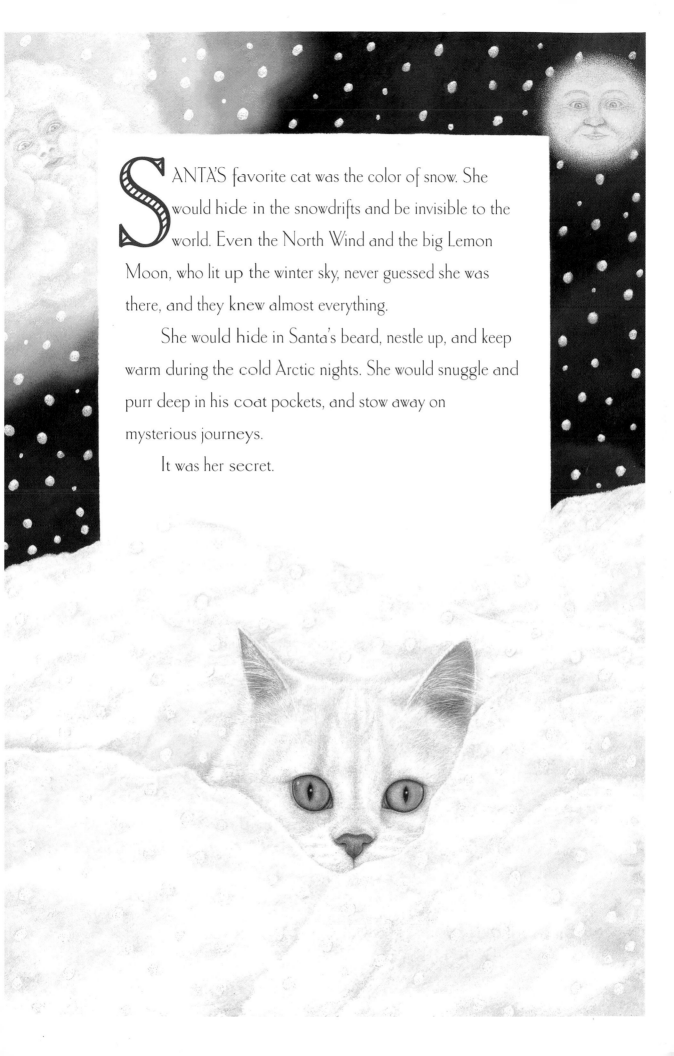

SANTA'S favorite cat was the color of snow. She
would hide in the snowdrifts and be invisible to the
world. Even the North Wind and the big Lemon
Moon, who lit up the winter sky, never guessed she was
there, and they knew almost everything.

She would hide in Santa's beard, nestle up, and keep
warm during the cold Arctic nights. She would snuggle and
purr deep in his coat pockets, and stow away on
mysterious journeys.

It was her secret.

SANTA called her Snow Cat, but this whitest of cats had the greenest of eyes, and in the moonlight her eyes would gleam the color of jade. That was just how the North Wind found out about his new playmate.

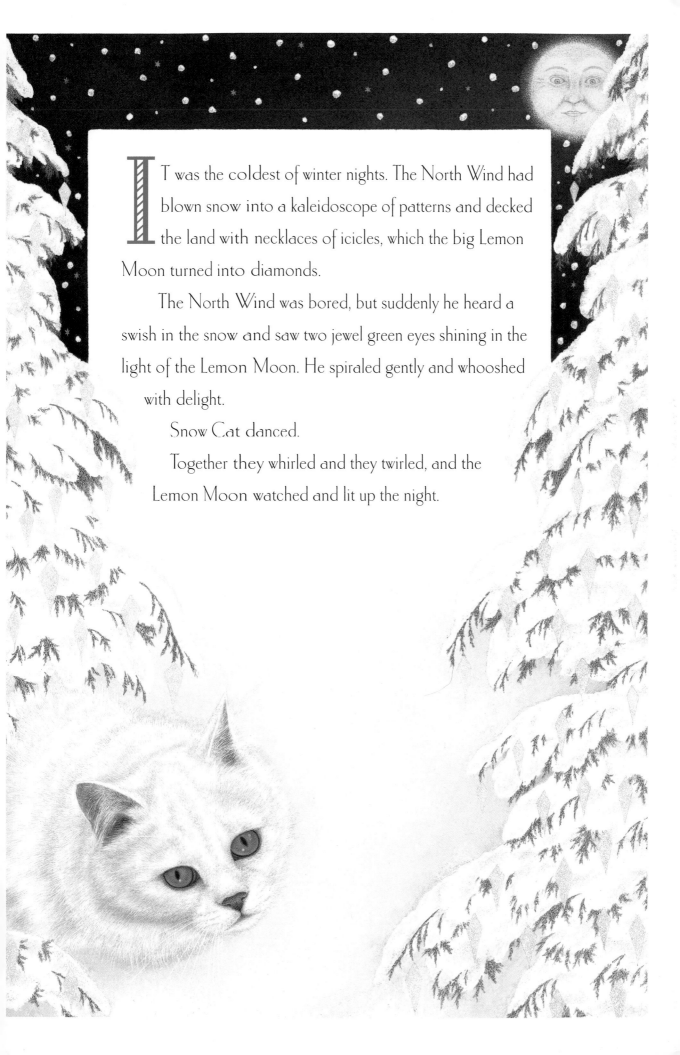

IT was the coldest of winter nights. The North Wind had blown snow into a kaleidoscope of patterns and decked the land with necklaces of icicles, which the big Lemon Moon turned into diamonds.

The North Wind was bored, but suddenly he heard a swish in the snow and saw two jewel green eyes shining in the light of the Lemon Moon. He spiraled gently and whooshed with delight.

Snow Cat danced.

Together they whirled and they twirled, and the Lemon Moon watched and lit up the night.

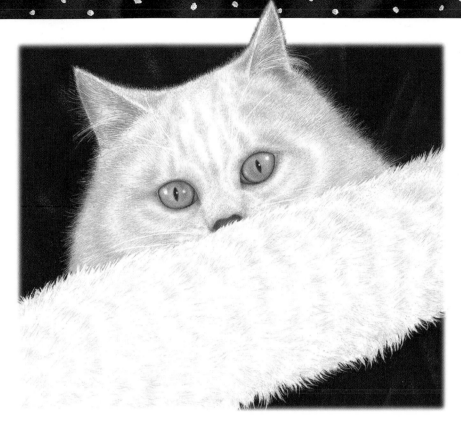

IT was the night before Christmas, and the Lemon Moon knew that it was time for a magical journey, so he lit the way for Snow Cat to go home. The North Wind huffed just a little and watched as she went into the icy, snowy house.

Secretly Snow Cat found the red snuggly, cuddly coat and crawled into a big, warm, furry pocket. Santa laughed a great happy laugh as he flung on his coat. "It's the night before Christmas!" Santa shouted.

In a jingle of bells and a flurry of snow they swished into the air.

Santa reached into his pocket for a mitten and found his Snow Cat. He pretended to be annoyed, but then he laughed.

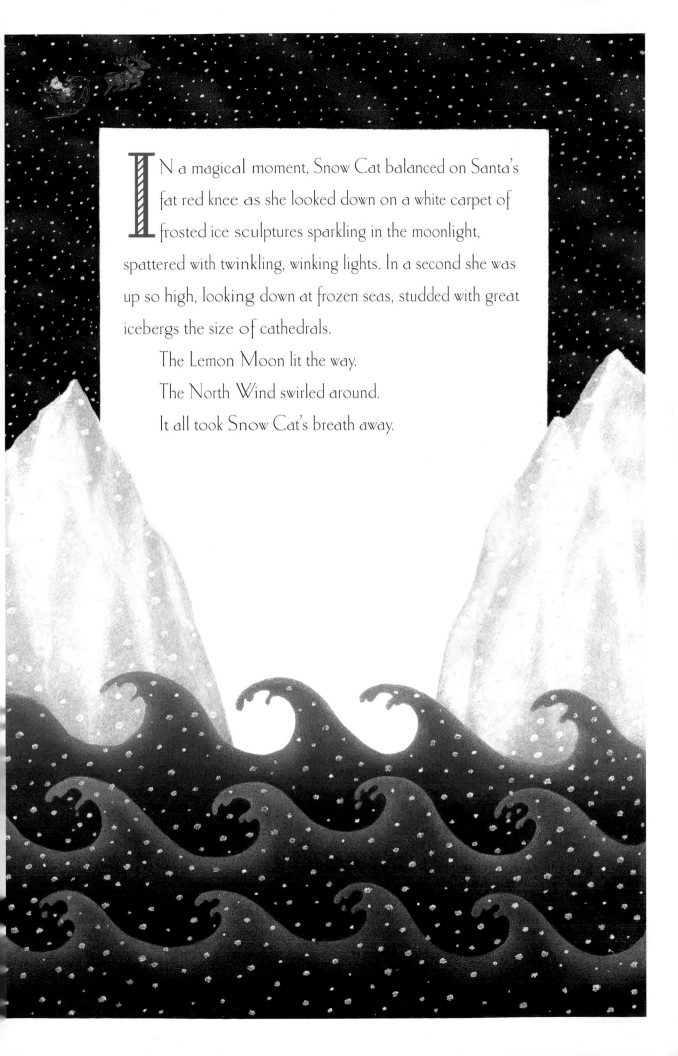

IN a magical moment, Snow Cat balanced on Santa's fat red knee as she looked down on a white carpet of frosted ice sculptures sparkling in the moonlight, spattered with twinkling, winking lights. In a second she was up so high, looking down at frozen seas, studded with great icebergs the size of cathedrals.

The Lemon Moon lit the way.

The North Wind swirled around.

It all took Snow Cat's breath away.

A MOMENT later, a mass of colored lights spiraled in a maze beneath her. Snow Cat shook her freezing whiskers and excitedly looked a little closer at the pattern of lights far below. She was enchanted. She twitched her nose and wondered what life was like down there—but then leaned too far. She fell.

Santa's big mittens tried to catch her. The North Wind tried to cushion her. The Lemon Moon closed his eyes. But Snow Cat still fell—tumbling, twisting, and turning toward the lights below. The North Wind carried Santa's words down to her: "Snow Cat, Snow Cat, my favorite cat, I will find you!"

S NOW Cat wondered where she had landed. There
were strange noises, flashing, brightly colored lights,
new smells, people chattering, traffic clanking, and
hustle and bustle everywhere.

She wanted to hide.

She had heard the cry and knew that Santa would be
looking for her. My Santa, I must find you, she thought.

Snow Cat trudged gingerly up the white street. Nimbly
she dodged people's feet—so many people. So many shoes,
so many different types of shoes. Some people spoke. "Hey,
pussycat," they said, but like quicksilver she avoided them.

NOW Snow Cat looked up, and towering above her were huge, tall buildings embossed with yellow lights that reached forever toward the starry, inky sky. Large snowflakes fell all around, but she couldn't see the Lemon Moon or hear the North Wind.

SUDDENLY she raced ahead to find herself nose-to-nose with Santa. Something was wrong. A nearly Santa, cold and bright, swinging slightly, beckoned her to a brightly lit store. Windows full of shimmering gold and silver swam before her eyes.

It wasn't her Santa. Despondently she moved on. Her paws were cold, her whiskers frozen.

ECHOING Christmas carols reached the confused ears of Snow Cat. She heard singing and calling, but when she looked up her eyes were glazed with flashing colors. She focused on a Santa all made of bright lights who was singing "Ho! Ho! Ho!"

It wasn't her Santa. Now it was snowing thickly. And where was the North Wind? The Lemon Moon was hiding, and it seemed that even the stars were asleep.

Surely her Santa could not be far away.

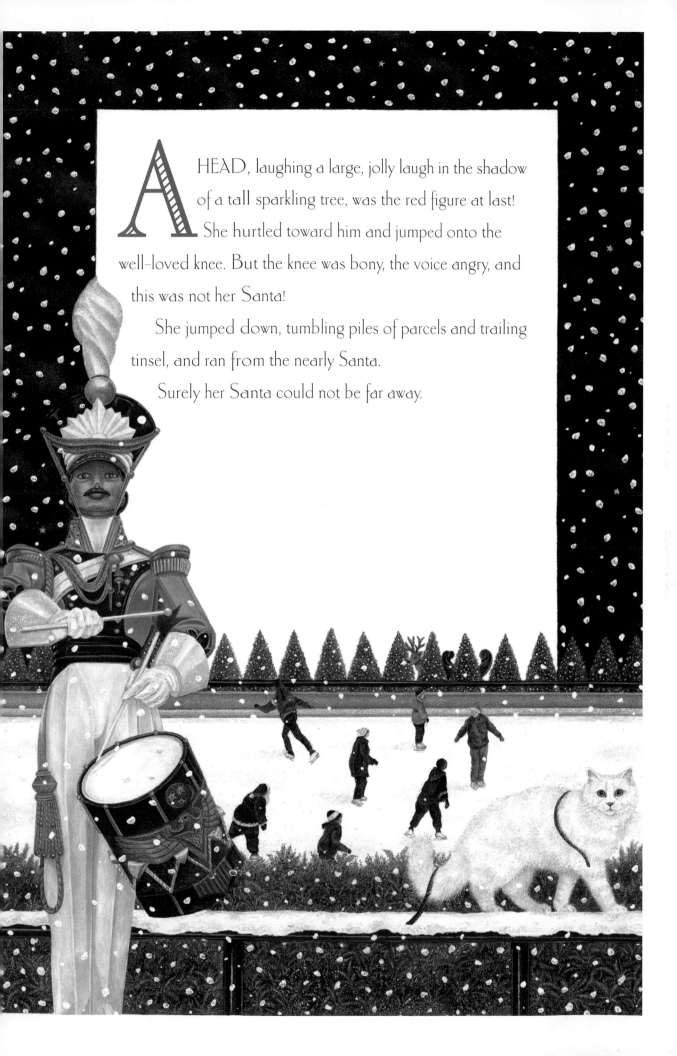

AHEAD, laughing a large, jolly laugh in the shadow
of a tall sparkling tree, was the red figure at last!
She hurtled toward him and jumped onto the
well-loved knee. But the knee was bony, the voice angry, and
this was not her Santa!

She jumped down, tumbling piles of parcels and trailing
tinsel, and ran from the nearly Santa.

Surely her Santa could not be far away.

THE night grew still as she waded through the new snow. People were busily disappearing into doorways. Snow Cat was desperate. Then, as she passed an old wooden door decorated with mistletoe and holly berries, she heard a familiar "Ho! Ho! Ho!" and wearily she squeezed in through a chink in the doorway.

THE house was warm and she followed the noise. Notes of festive music wafted in the air, and the scent of pine needles and oranges was everywhere.

As Snow Cat turned a corner, she had another shock. A smiling Santa was looking out from the flickering screen— another nearly Santa!

FRIGHTENED, she turned quickly and gently knocked the glittering tree. It twinkled, just as though it were laughing at her.

Snow Cat looked up, and a glass ball fell between her paws. She looked again, and saw that the glass ball was yet another nearly Santa, shining and smiling at her.

Snow Cat sank to the ground. She had given up. She slept with the littlest Santa between her paws.

It was not until much, much later that she awoke. She was now sure that her Santa had forgotten her.

IF only Snow Cat had known that Santa and his sleigh
had spiraled down wildly after her and had landed on
the tallest of tall buildings.

Santa was still searching, along with the North Wind
and the big Lemon Moon.

SNOW Cat awoke in the nighttime glint of the
Christmas lights. The house was so quiet, so still.
Her ears twitched and picked up a sound far away,
then her whiskers twitched, then her nose twitched. A moment
later—to a sound of clumping and guffawing—she was
looking at big, black, snowy boots and up at a fat, snuggly,
cuddly coat. And was that her big, warm, furry pocket?

Could it be Santa?

"Snow Cat! My best Christmas present," Santa whispered.
He scooped her up and laughed his great jolly laugh.

THAT night the North Wind blew a homeward path in the falling snow for Santa and his favorite cat. Since that Christmas, Santa always travels with his Snow Cat, and sometimes, even now, they are glimpsed on the tallest of tall buildings.

Santa's Snow Cat

Text copyright © 2001 by Sue Stainton

Illustrations copyright © 2001 by Anne Mortimer

Manufactured in China. All rights reserved. No part of this book may
be used or reproduced in any manner whatsoever without written
permission except in the case of brief quotations embodied in critical
articles and reviews. For information address HarperCollins Children's
Books, a division of HarperCollins Publishers, 1350 Avenue of the
Americas, New York, NY 10019.

www.harpercollinschildrens.com

Library of Congress Cataloging-in-Publication Data
Stainton, Sue.
Santa's Snow Cat / by Sue Stainton ; illustrations by Anne Mortimer.—
1st ed.
p.   cm.
Summary: Santa and his favorite cat search for each other after she falls
out of his sleigh and lands in New York City on Christmas Eve.
ISBN 978-0-06-623827-2 (trade bdg.)
ISBN 978-0-06-623828-9 (lib. bdg.)
ISBN 978-0-06-000540-5 (pbk.)
[1. Cats—Fiction. 2. Santa Claus—Fiction. 3. Christmas—Fiction.
4. Lost and found possessions—Fiction. 5. New York (N.Y.)—Fiction.]
I. Mortimer, Anne, ill. II. Title.
PZ7.S782555 San 2001

[E]—dc21   2001024163

Typography by Al Cetta

First Edition

Also by Sue Stainton and Anne Mortimer

Praise for THE LIGHTHOUSE CAT:

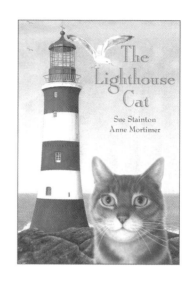

"This clever interweaving of two popular picture-book subjects, cats and lighthouses, is enlivened with Mortimer's gleaming illustrations, which literally shine."
—*Kirkus Reviews*

"This beautifully illustrated tale is set in the past, when a lighthouse was lit with a 24-candle lantern and the keeper was responsible for trimming the wicks every half hour. Stainton tells how a lonely keeper discovers a stray cat on board the supply boat and decides to keep him. Mackerel proves to be the perfect companion for the man, helping him to watch for boats and providing company at night. When a terrible storm knocks out the lantern and the keeper is unable to re-light it, Mackerel prevents a shipwreck by summoning 11 of his feline friends. The close-up renderings of the gray-coated, green-eyed cat are especially appealing. This is a great book for children to read for personal enjoyment and for teachers to share." —*School Library Journal*

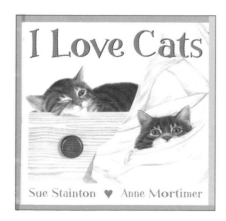

I LOVE CATS

"This picture book has what every cat person wants—a lot of felines in all their playful, mysterious glory. Mortimer's cats are second to none. The repetitive, rhyming text, use of opposites, and buoyant pictures make this a good selection for early readers."
—*School Library Journal*

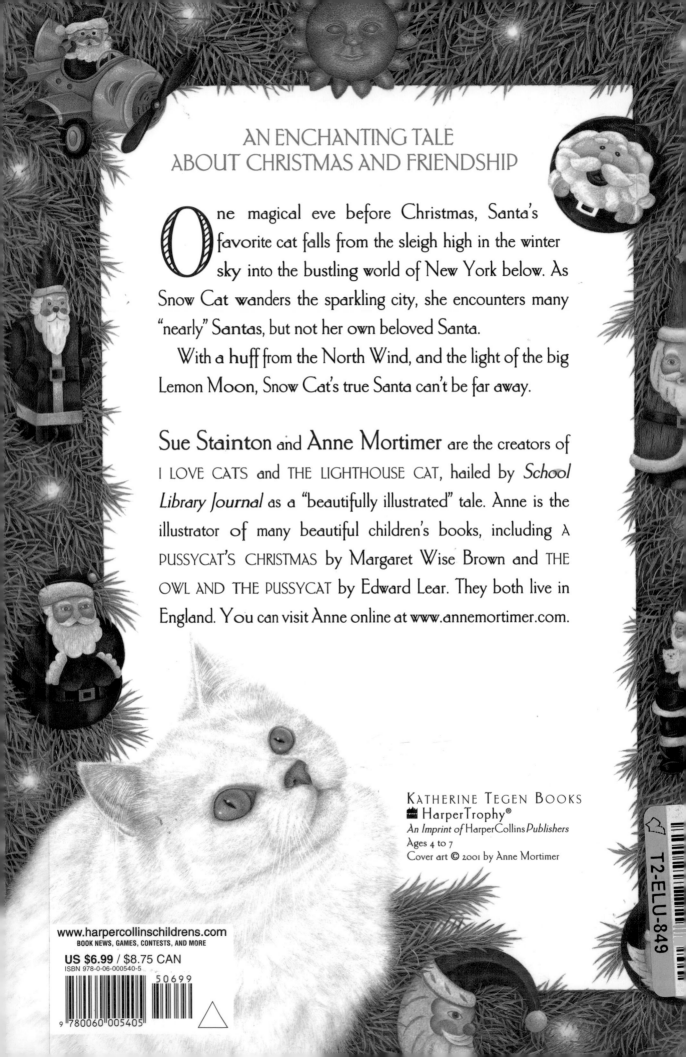

AN ENCHANTING TALE ABOUT CHRISTMAS AND FRIENDSHIP

One magical eve before Christmas, Santa's favorite cat falls from the sleigh high in the winter sky into the bustling world of New York below. As Snow Cat wanders the sparkling city, she encounters many "nearly" Santas, but not her own beloved Santa.

With a huff from the North Wind, and the light of the big Lemon Moon, Snow Cat's true Santa can't be far away.

Sue Stainton and **Anne Mortimer** are the creators of I LOVE CATS and THE LIGHTHOUSE CAT, hailed by *School Library Journal* as a "beautifully illustrated" tale. Anne is the illustrator of many beautiful children's books, including A PUSSYCAT'S CHRISTMAS by Margaret Wise Brown and THE OWL AND THE PUSSYCAT by Edward Lear. They both live in England. You can visit Anne online at www.annemortimer.com.

KATHERINE TEGEN BOOKS
HarperTrophy®
An Imprint of HarperCollins *Publishers*
Ages 4 to 7
Cover art © 2001 by Anne Mortimer